W9-DAD-299

WEST GA REG LIB SYS
Neva Lomason
Memorial Library
DISCARD

Long Was the Winter Road They Traveled

A TALE OF THE NATIVITY

J. Patrick Lewis • pictures by Drew Bairley

Dial Books for Young Readers New York

Published by Dial Books for Young Readers
A Division of Penguin Books USA Inc.
375 Hudson Street
New York, New York 10014
Text copyright © 1997 by J. Patrick Lewis
Pictures copyright © 1997 by Drew Bairley
All rights reserved
Designed by Nancy R. Leo
Printed in Hong Kong
First Edition
1 3 5 7 9 10 8 6 4 2

Library of Congress Cataloging in Publication Data
Lewis, J. Patrick.
Long was the winter road they traveled: a tale of the nativity /
J. Patrick Lewis; pictures by Drew Bairley.
p.   cm.
ISBN 0-8037-1814-4 (tr. bdg.).—ISBN 0-8037-1815-2 (lib. bdg.)
1. Jesus Christ—Nativity—Juvenile poetry. 2. Children's poetry, American.
3. Christmas—Juvenile poetry. 4. Animals—Juvenile poetry.
[1. Jesus Christ—Nativity—Poetry. 2. American poetry. 3. Christmas—Poetry.
4. Animals—Poetry.] I. Bairley, Drew, ill. II. Title.
PS3562.E9465L66 1997   811'.54—DC20   94-35680   CIP   AC

The art was rendered in oil.
The underpainting of each piece is an oil and sand composition.

To Patti Rothermich, Jay Kegley, Wendy Ramsey,
and to all the librarians, past and present,
at Otterbein College's Courtright Memorial Library
J.P.L.

With special appreciation to Kate Pollex, Jeff Hartle,
John Pollex, Alex Baer, and Zachary Denomy

D.B.

Long was the winter road they traveled.
Long after darkness fell
On Bethlehem, Mary and Joseph,
Turned out of a cold hotel,

Had settled themselves in a stable,
Where many a footpath ran—
For Bird and Beast, for Kings of the East—
To the little caravan.

The flute of a Cuckoo piped music
On the rump of Burro Brown,
And a Spider wrote an enchanting note
On the hem of Mary's gown.

The Sheep coughed low, the Sheepdog
Softly encircled the Lamb.
A star shone down on the children
Of the children of Abraham.

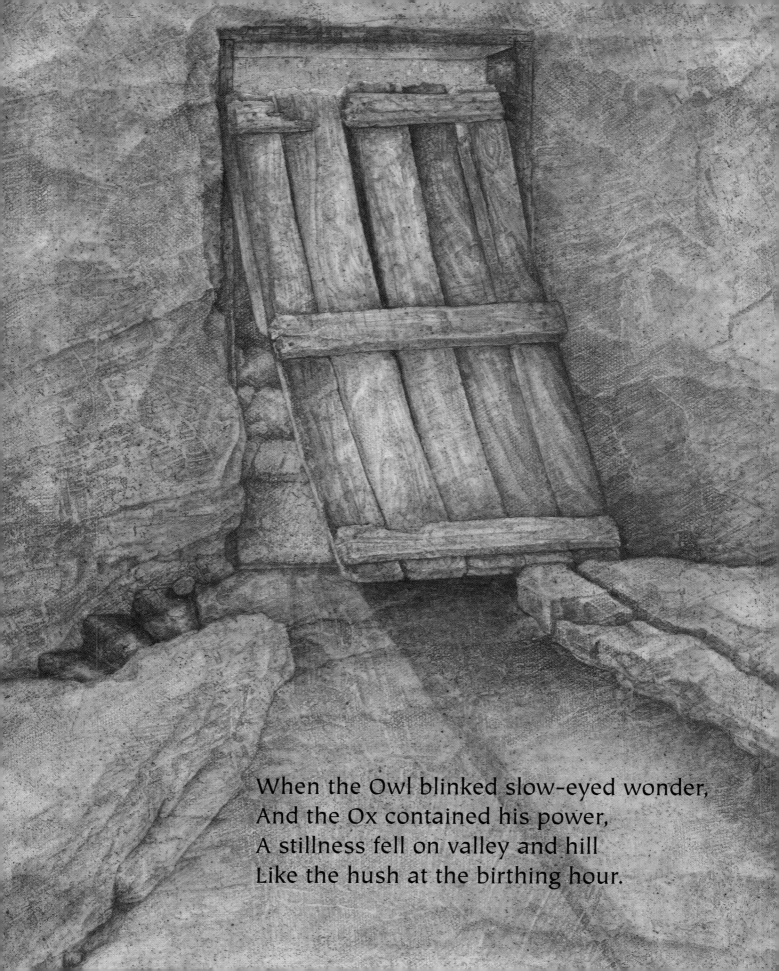

When the Owl blinked slow-eyed wonder,
And the Ox contained his power,
A stillness fell on valley and hill
Like the hush at the birthing hour.

The wood fire flare tinseled the air!
Two rafter Bats, light-shy,
Stirred . . . curious. The Chanticleer
Was first to hear His cry.

Jackrabbit delighted Jack Jackal.
Jerusalem Crickets spread
"Joy to the Fields"—a Cricket carol.
The Dormouse bowed his head.

By the Cat who velveted evening
Sat the Crow who blackened night—
Together Old Feather-and-Fur beheld
The Mother in half-moon light.

Camels, emperors of the desert,
Bellied down, murmuring steam.
A Goat—o brave the whisker-gray—
Watched the Infant Jesus dream.

The Milk Cow mooed as if to say
How beautiful to the Mare,
Who whinnied *Oh*. And frankincense
Curled in the turning air.

Then Joseph said, "Go, all of you
Who grace the blessed Earth,
To every Sister and Brother Beast—
Tell them you marked His birth."

And many were the Birds who flew
To Hebron and Jericho.
And many were the Beasts who knew
What all the world would know.

The stable doorway creaked farewell.
On hoof and wing they went,
Bellowing, bleating . . . or perfectly still
In their astonishment.

A great green rush of Hummingbirds
Unfolded into flight
With news of the Nativity
This thousand-angeled night.

When morning broke on Bethlehem,
A phantom wind would blow
His message—crystal clear—that falls
On blessed Christmas . . . snow.

Long was the winter road they traveled :
J 811.54 LEWIS   740899

Lewis, J. Patrick.
    WEST GEORGIA REGIONAL LIBRARY